P9-ELT-468

For Gillian, Kathleen, and Mark,
my brilliant, funny, good sweeties.
My wishes come true.

Copyright © 2011 by Carolyn Conahan.
All rights reserved.
No part of this publication may be reproduced in any form
without written permission from the publisher.

Library of Congress Cataloging-in-Publication Data
Conahan, Carolyn.
The big wish / by Carolyn Conahan.
p. cm.
Summary: A young girl tries to make a world record–breaking wish.
ISBN 978-0-8118-7040-5 (alk. paper)
[1. Wishes—Fiction. 2. World records—Fiction.] I. Title.
PZ7.C746Bi 2011
[E]—dc22
2010027353

Book design by Kristine Brogno.
Typeset in Usherwood.
The illustrations in this book were rendered in watercolor.

Manufactured by Toppan Leefung, Da Ling Shan Town,
Dongguan, China, in January 2011.

1 3 5 7 9 10 8 6 4 2

This product conforms to CPSIA 2008.

Chronicle Books LLC
680 Second Street, San Francisco, California 94107

www.chroniclekids.com

The Big Wish

Carolyn Conahan

chronicle books · san francisco

Molly's yard was all dandelions, from side to side to side. Dandelions crowded the steps to the house like they wanted in. Dandelions leaned through the fence like they wanted out.

Snip-snip! Clip-clip! Molly's neighbor, Pie, pushed his mower to the gate. "My Granny says to ask if I can mow your weeds."

"Weeds are a public nuisance," said Granny Perkins, who was also the mayor.

"These are NOT weeds," said Molly. "I'm growing a big wish. A World Record Wish!"

Pie squinted. "Like in the book, for real?"

Molly nodded. "I wrote to them. They're waiting for my call."

"Let's call 'em now!" said Pie.

But the dandelions weren't ready.

"I have to keep them safe until they turn into wish-puffs." Molly sighed. "I also need to pick a wish."

"I'd wish for my own superpowers," said Pie. "OR a dinosaur."

"I'd wish for a unicorn," said Pie's sister, Poppy. "No, a flying unicorn!"

Molly wondered, "Should a World Record Wish be for just one person?"

"Let's have a contest for the biggest, best wish!" said Pie. "Molly can pick."

"A World Record would put this town on the map," said Granny Perkins. "I must contact the media."

The library could use a new book-mobile...
I've always dreamed of being a Star on the stage.
Beep! Beep!
Farmer's Market
Wish Here!
Today

Banners, posters, and big boxes marked WISH HERE! appeared all over town.

And all over town, people wished.

Some people wished in crayon.
Some people wished in ink.

Some people wished on scraps of paper folded so small they almost disappeared.

Molly sat with her dandelions and read every wish.
Every one by one by one.

Wishes for pets and friends and family. For long-lost things and longed-for things. Things to do. Things to be. Sad wishes. Hopeful wishes. Sloppy, sappy, smoochy wishes.

"So many wishes!" said Pie.

Molly's dandelions nodded and turned to wish-puffs, one by one by one.

"Don't forget the World Record," said Granny Perkins. "We need that wish."

How could Molly forget? It was all anyone talked about, everywhere she went.

“We need one BIG wish,” said Pie.

“For the Record,” said Granny Perkins.

“For the WORLD,” said Poppy.

Angus Crumpet hugged a book to his heart. “Let’s wish for knowledge. Wisdom for all.”

“A world full of singing. Dancing. Joy!” Buzz Pumpkin twirled on his toes.

“Oh!” said Ms. Lottie Sparks. “We could wish the world clean and safe for whales, and wombats, and meerkats, and mole rats, AND bugs, AND birds, AND people.”

“No!” cried Granny Perkins. “We should wish away poverty, hunger, and disease. We should wish away WAR.”

“Now THAT’S a big wish,” said Pie.

“That’s more than ONE wish,” said Molly.

Poppy sighed. “Could we still have unicorns?”

“Please,” said Granny Perkins. “This is important.”

“Fun is important.” Buzz Pumpkin thumped his fist. “Joy is important!”

“MISTER Pumpkin,” said Granny Perkins, “do you really wish to wish joy to the world?”

"Don't fight over the wish!" cried Molly.

"They're your dandelions," said Pie. "You get to pick the wish."

Everyone looked at Molly.

Molly squirmed. "Let's see if the dandelions are ready."

They were! The dandelions had all become wish-puffs.
They danced on their stalks and stretched to catch the wind.

Poink! A cold, hard something bounced off Molly's head.
Rain? No, hail! Hail would pound the wish-puffs flat . . .

"Help!" cried Molly.

Townsfolk ran for umbrellas, blankets, sheets, and tarps. They covered Molly's yard from side to side to side as the hailstorm rushed at them, flinging and stinging.

When the storm finally blew over and away, the crowd stepped back. The wish-puffs had been saved! Everyone cheered. Suddenly, Molly knew what to do. She marched inside to call the World Record Officials.

Before long, shiny trucks rumbled into town. Officials sprang out to mark and measure and count. Granny Perkins showed the media where to catch all the action. The town band assembled. Tuned up. Fell silent.

Molly invited everyone to pick a wish-puff. Pie first, then the rest. Old and young, neighbors and strangers, dogs, cats, chickens and all.

Molly picked the last puff. The crowd crowded closer.

"Thank you for sharing your wishes. I tried to pick the biggest, best one . . ." Molly took a deep breath. "I couldn't do it. I'm sorry."

The crowd gasped.

Molly stood tall. "I don't know if it will make a record, but if you don't mind, think of a wish. Your own big wish!

We'll wish together. One . . . **two** . . . **three** . . ."

"wish!"

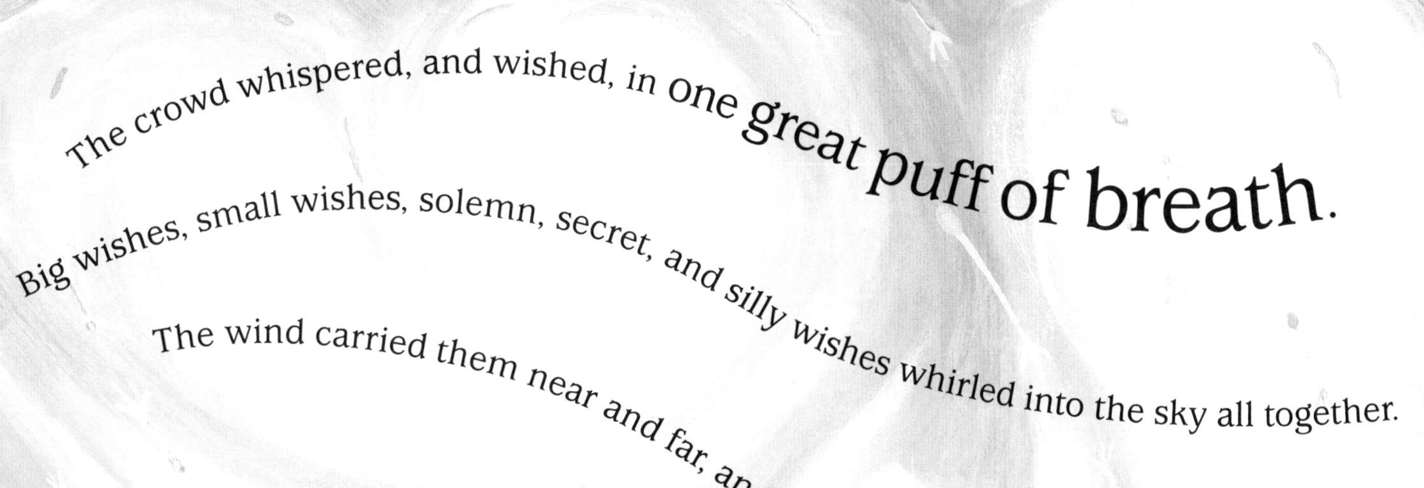

The crowd whispered, and wished, in one great puff of breath.

Big wishes, small wishes, solemn, secret, and silly wishes whirled into the sky all together.

The wind carried them near and far, and farther still, out of sight, across the world.

We're in the book- all of us!
VrrooM!
Yay, Molly!
Angus Crumpet's Books to Go!
We're Famous!
A wish is just the beginning, of course. There's still so much to do! (Do be careful to get my good side...)

It was the biggest wish event ever.
A World Record!

AND THAT'S OFFICIAL.

E FICTION CONAHAN
Conahan, Carolyn.
The big wish /

QT EFC L8900825 c2011.